Chapter One

Emergency Fighter

Our class is visiting a **fire station**.
We want to find out what a **firefighter** does.
We meet Jim the firefighter.

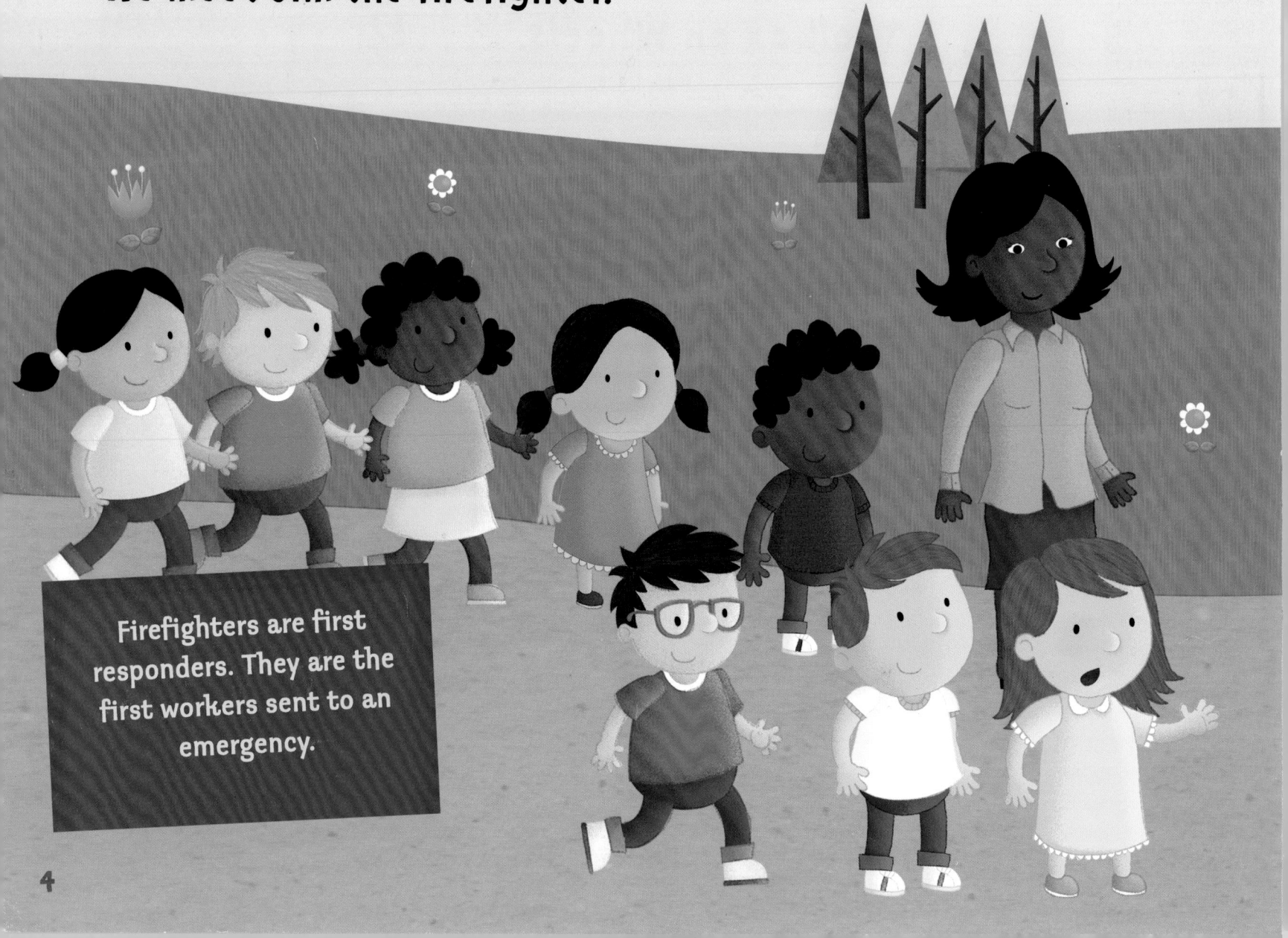

Firefighters are first responders. They are the first workers sent to an emergency.

TABLE OF CONTENTS

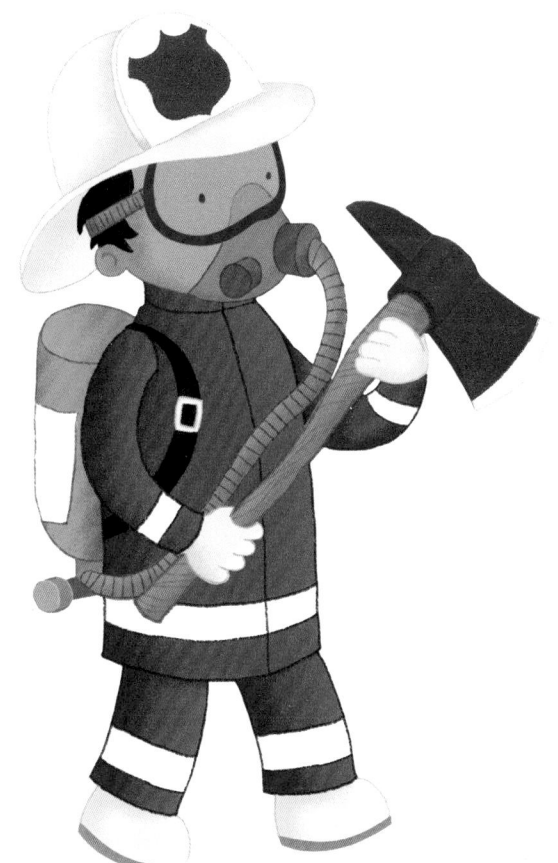

For firefighting heroes—G.B.
To Pat and Dean —E.M.

Millbrook Press
A division of Lerner Publishing Group, Inc.
241 First Avenue North
Minneapolis, MN 55401 U.S.A.

Website address: www.lernerbooks.com

Main body text set in Slappy Inline 18/28.
Typeface provided by T26.

Library of Congress Cataloging-in-Publication Data

Bellisario, Gina.
    Let's meet a firefighter / by Gina Bellisario ; illustrated by
Ed Myer.
      p.   cm. — (Cloverleaf Books : community helpers)
    Includes index.
    ISBN: 978-0-7613-9025-1 (lib. bdg. : alk. paper)
    1. Fire fighters—Juvenile literature. I. Title.
HD8039.F5.B45 2013
363.37—dc23   2012022479

Manufactured in the United States of America
1 – BP – 12/31/12

M MILLBROOK PRESS · MINNEAPOLIS

Gina Bellisario
illustrated by Ed Myer

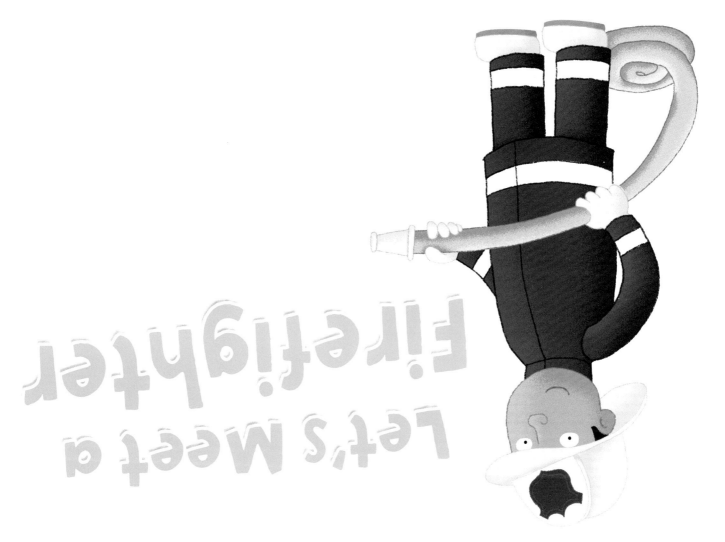

Let's Meet a Firefighter

cloverleaf books™

Community Helpers

"I solve problems called **emergencies**," says Firefighter Jim.

"Does that mean you put out fires?" asks Juliana.

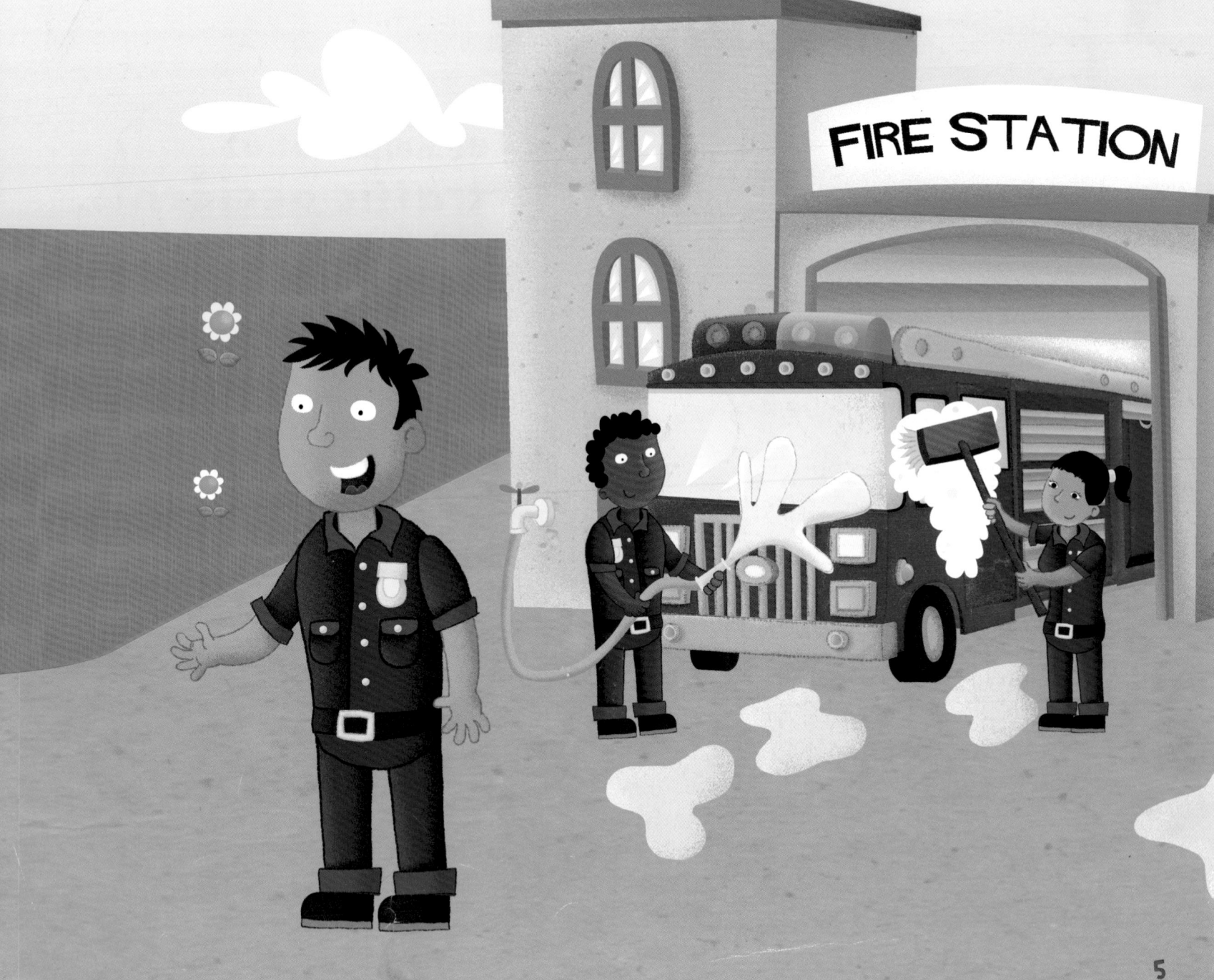

Firefighter Jim says he does a lot more than **fight fires.**

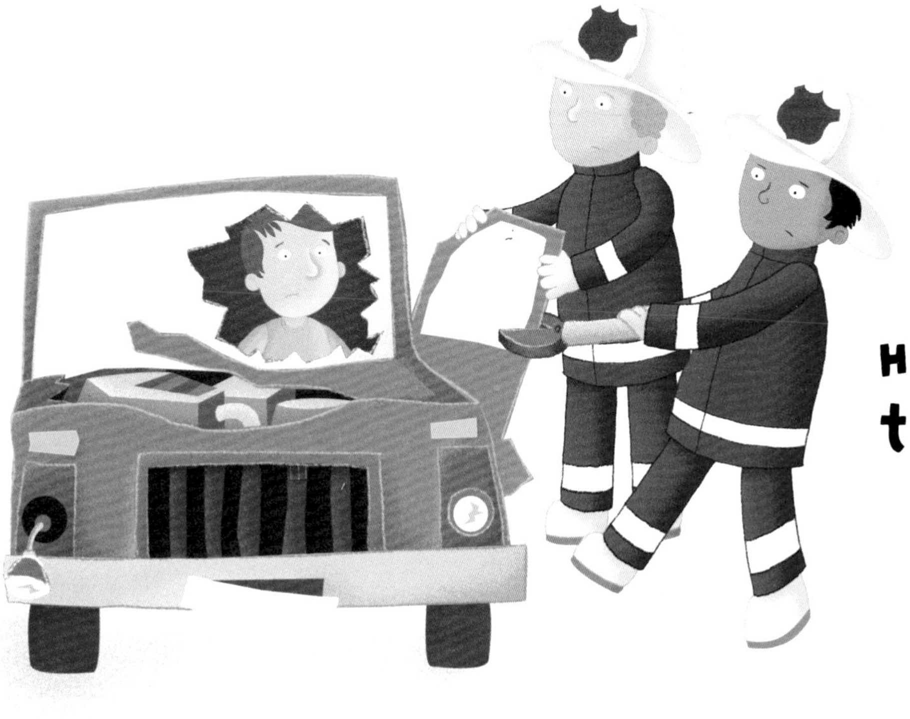

He helps out at
traffic accidents.

He **rescues** people
trapped by floods.

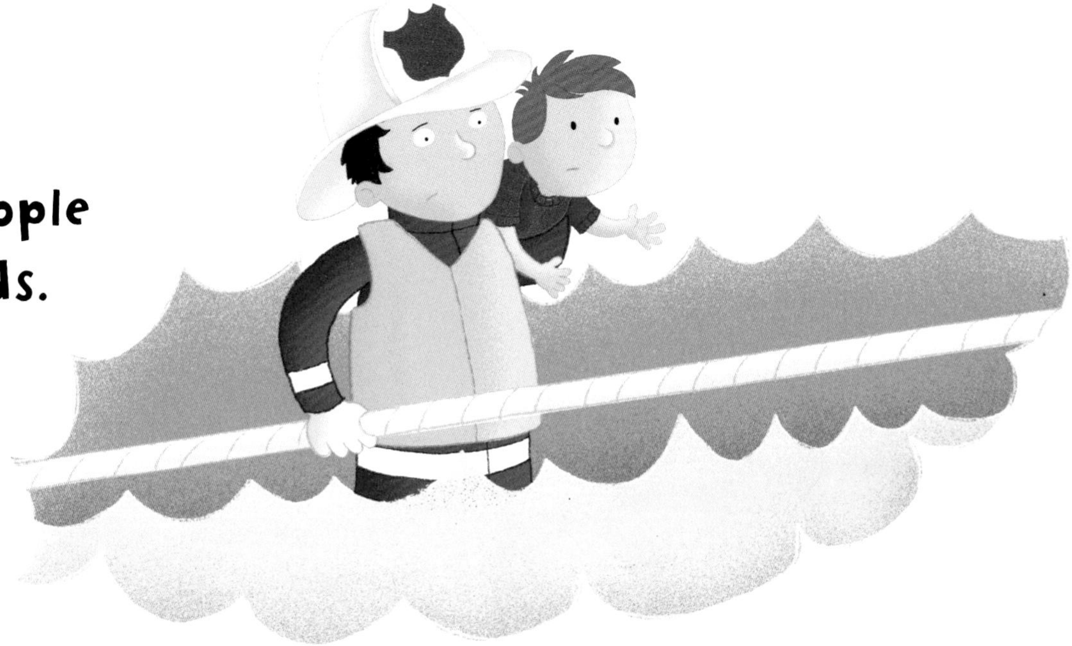

But mostly, he deals with **medical emergencies.** Sometimes people who are sick or hurt need help fast. A fire department ambulance can often get there the fastest.

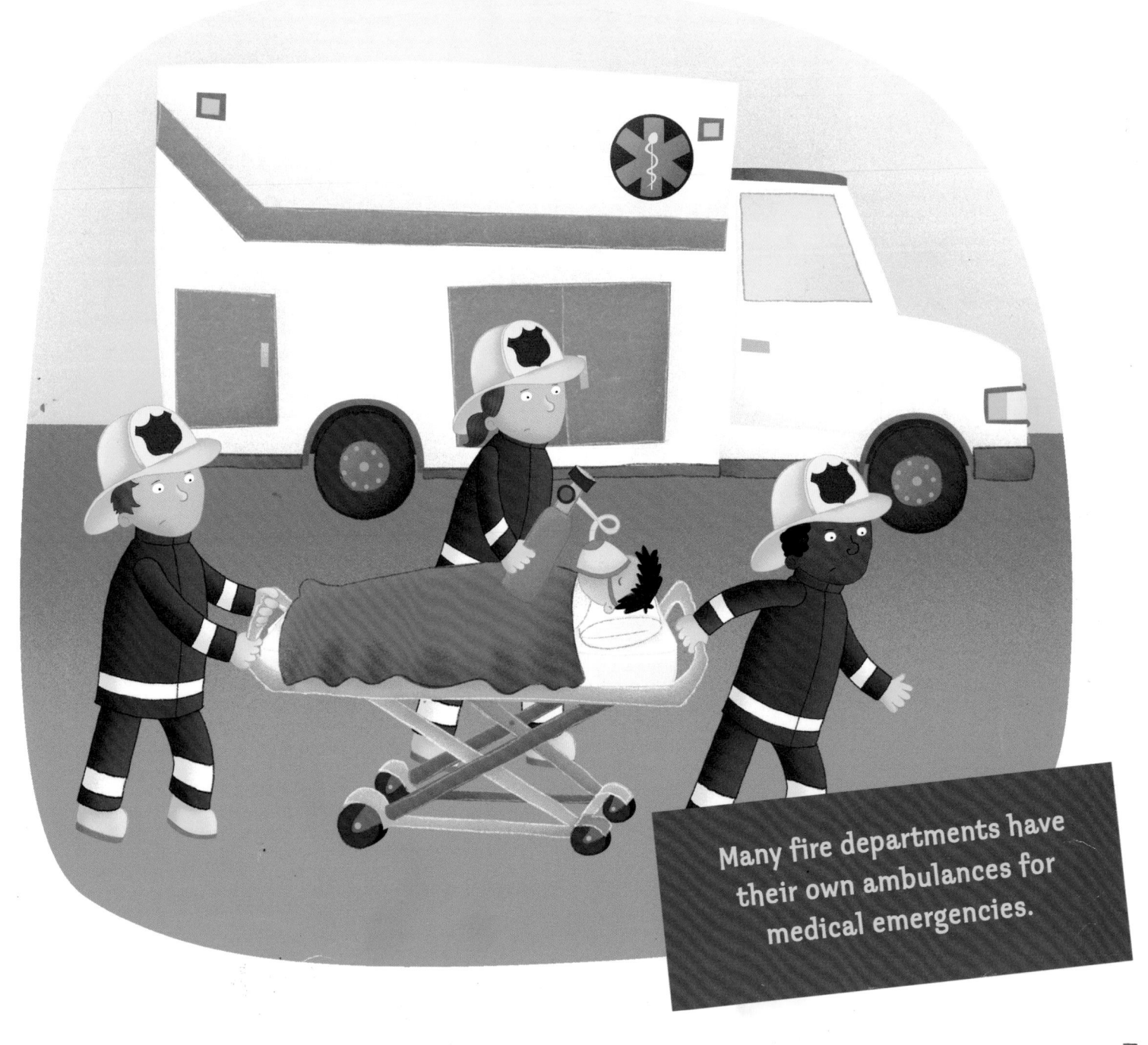

Many fire departments have their own ambulances for medical emergencies.

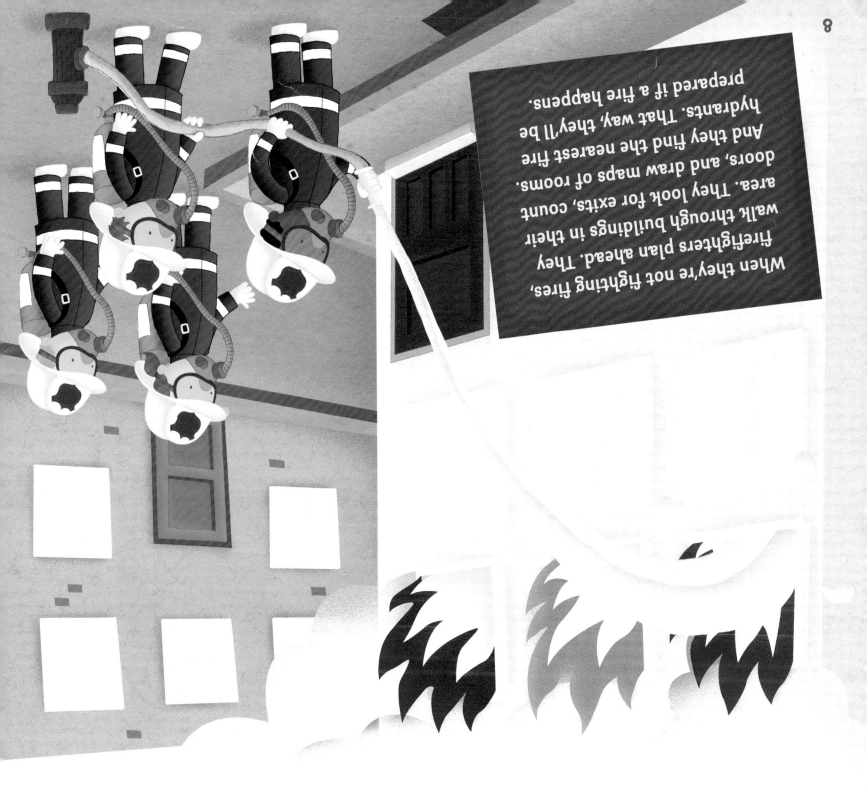

When they're not fighting fires, firefighters plan ahead. They walk through buildings in their area. They look for exits, count doors, and draw maps of rooms. And they find the nearest fire hydrants. That way, they'll be prepared if a fire happens.

Firefighters also fight plenty of fires. They put out fires in buildings and **save people** in danger.

These fires burn in forests and fields.

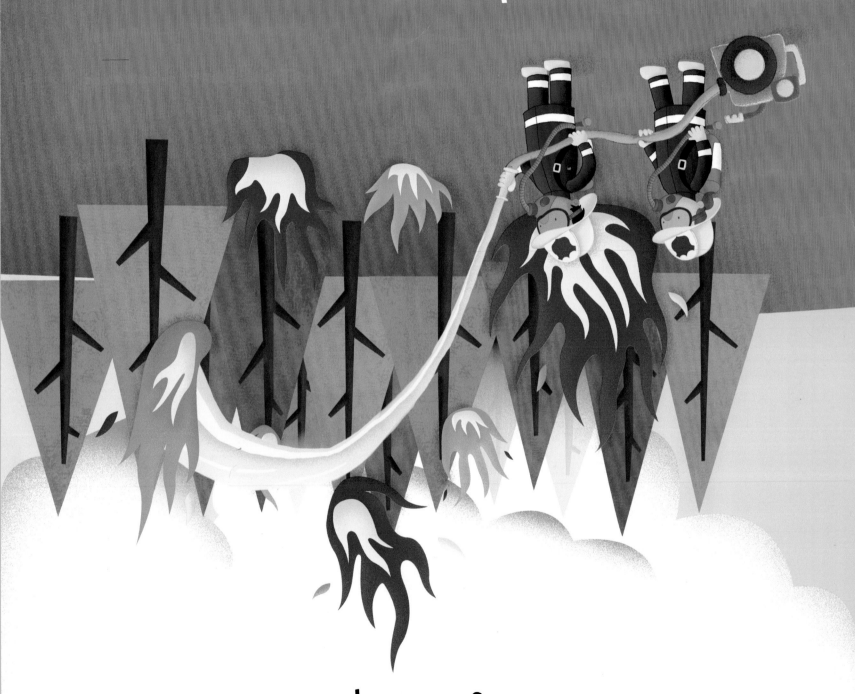

Some firefighters stop wildfires.

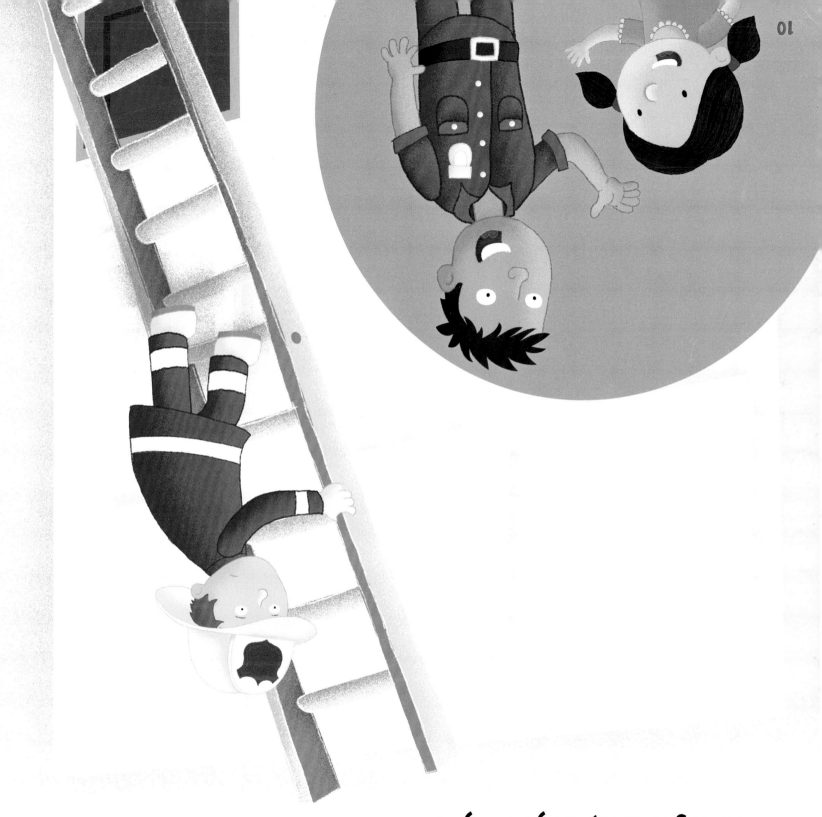

"When I grow up, I want to help people in emergencies," says Maya.

"That's what I said too," says Firefighter Jim. "After high school, I went to a **fire academy**. I learned how firefighters do their job. Then I became a firefighter."

"You mean an emergency fighter!" says Maya.

All firefighters must learn life-saving skills. They get first aid training. They practice caring for wounded people and giving medicine. Many firefighters also learn how to handle more serious medical emergencies.

Chapter Two

Toolbox on Wheels

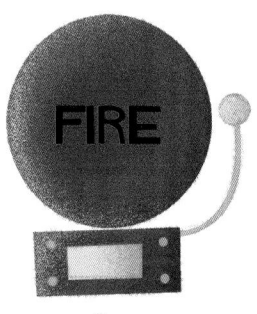

Firefighter Jim uses rescue tools for emergencies. He keeps the tools inside his fire truck.

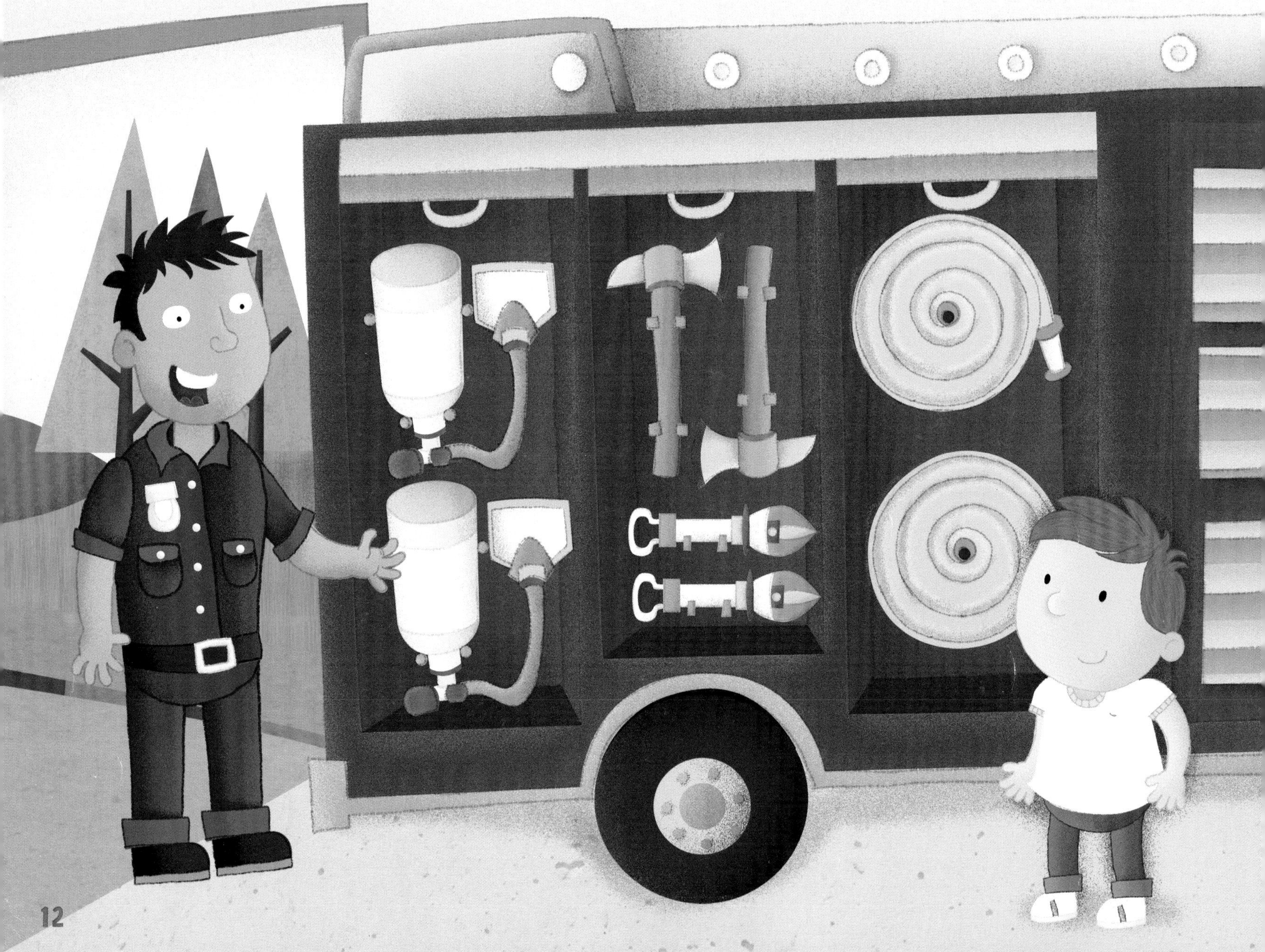

An **ax** opens windows. A **fire hose** carries water. Jim's **air pack** holds oxygen. A fire can fill a room with smoke. The pack gives Jim clean air. He breathes the air through a mask on his face.

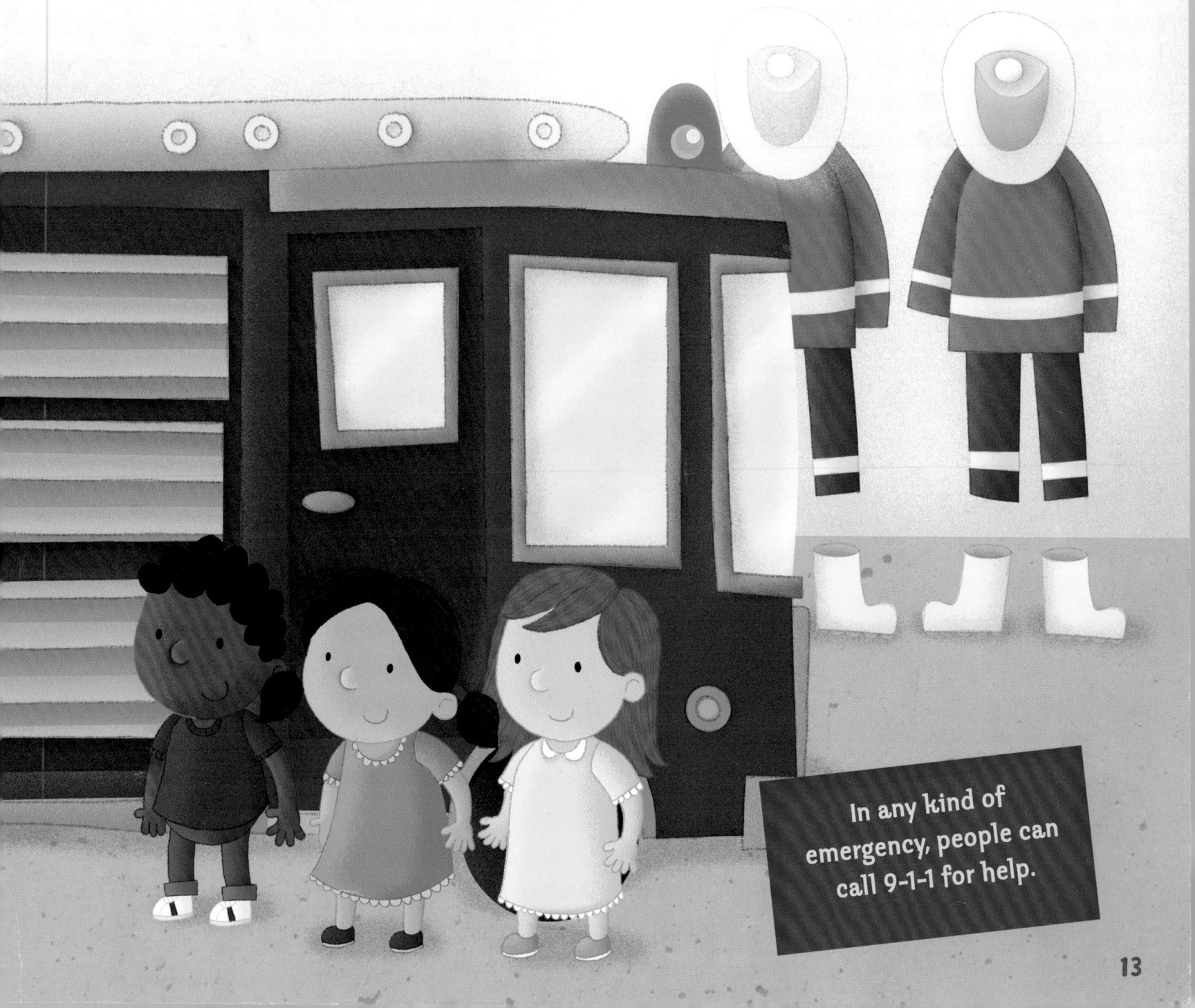

In any kind of emergency, people can call 9-1-1 for help.

13

"I wear the air pack with my firefighting clothes," says Firefighter Jim. Firefighting clothes are called **bunker gear.**

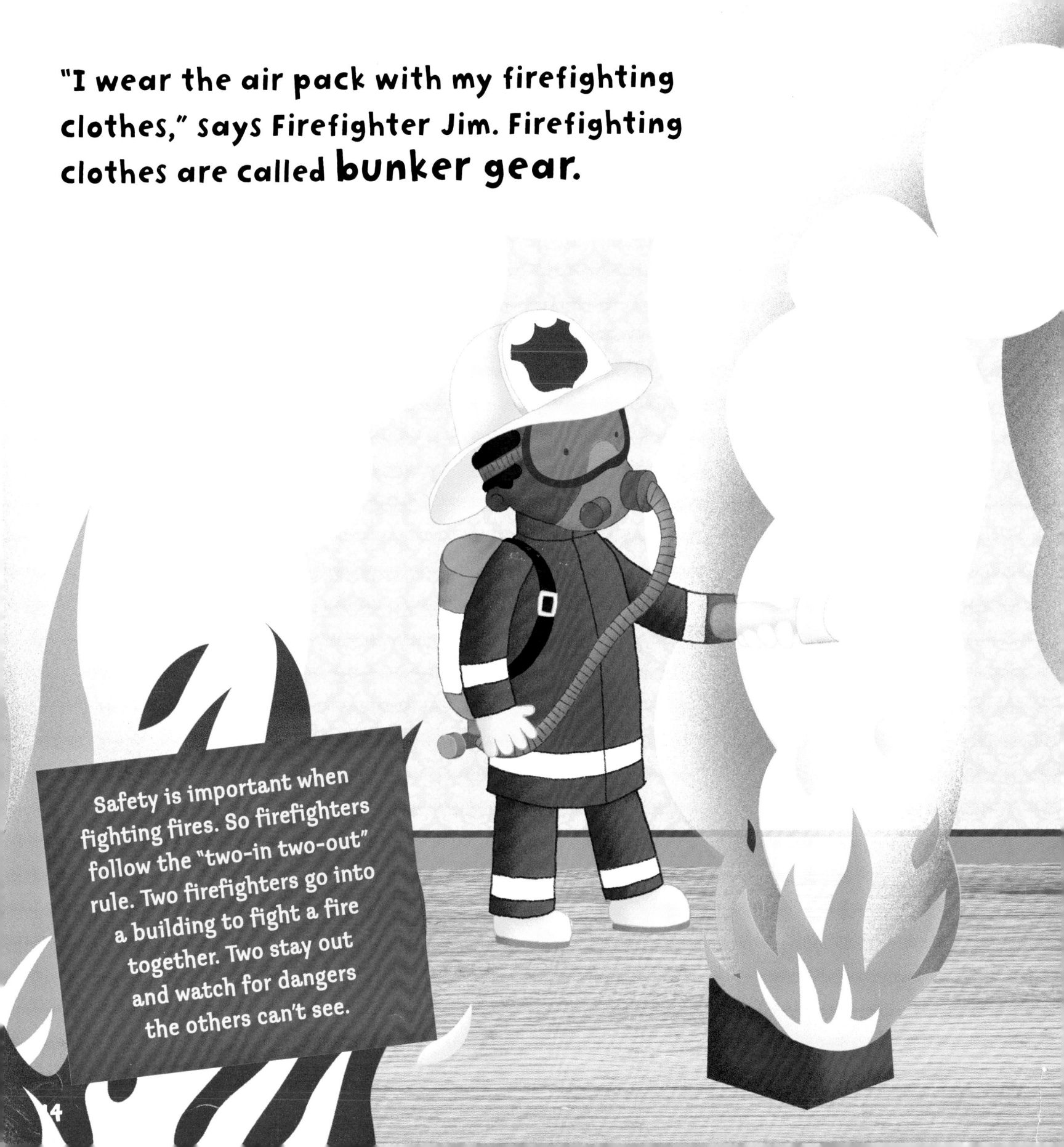

Safety is important when fighting fires. So firefighters follow the "two-in two-out" rule. Two firefighters go into a building to fight a fire together. Two stay out and watch for dangers the others can't see.

14

Special pants and coats protect Jim against burns. This bunker gear keeps him safe in fires up to 500°F (260°C).

That's hotter than most ovens!

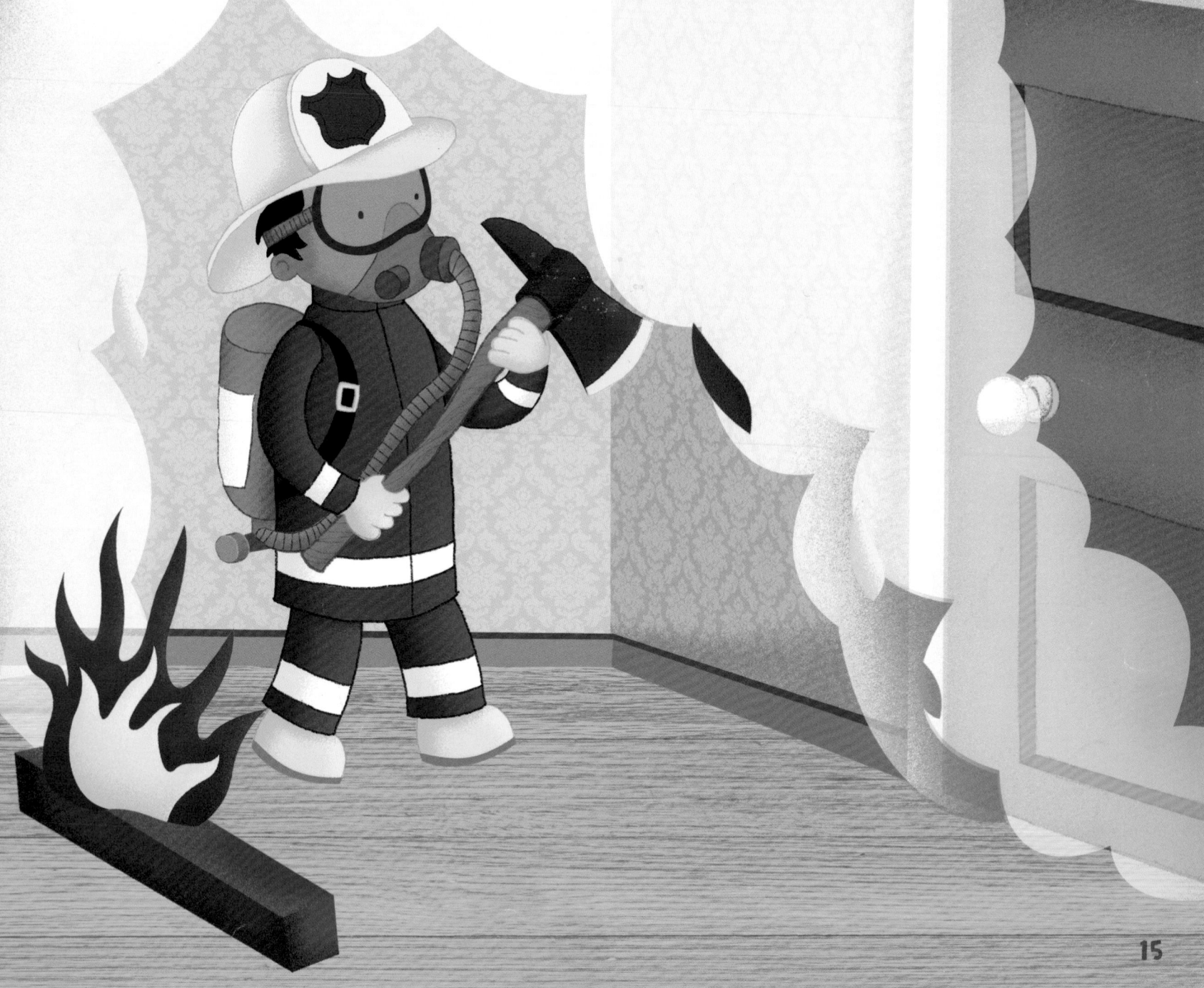

A fire truck is a tool too.

It is also called a hook and ladder truck.

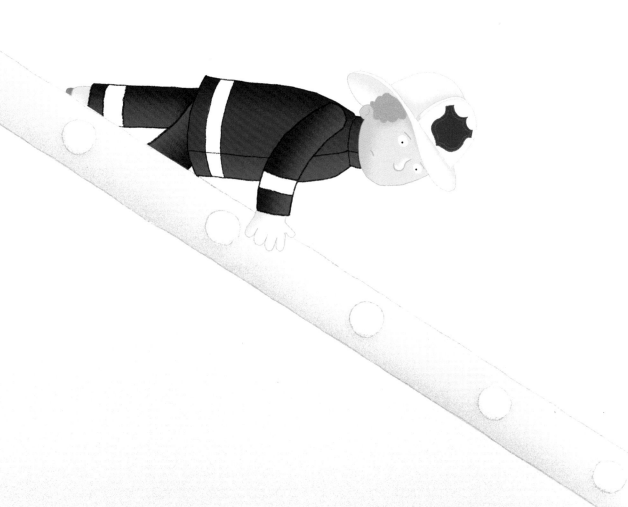

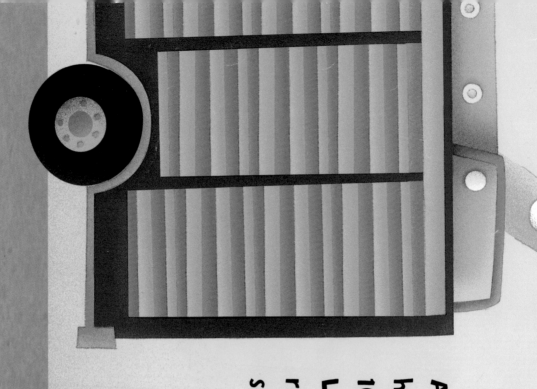

A metal ladder on top helps firefighters climb 100 feet (30 meters) high. Ladder hooks latch onto a roof. They keep the ladder steady against a building.

Taking care of tools is an important part of a firefighter's job. Firefighters clean trucks and other supplies. They wash their fire equipment. Broken hoses That way, their tools are replaced. ready for the next rescue.

Chapter Three

Community Hero

Firefighter Jim is more than an emergency fighter. He teaches the community about **fire safety**. Gavin thinks that makes Jim a hero.

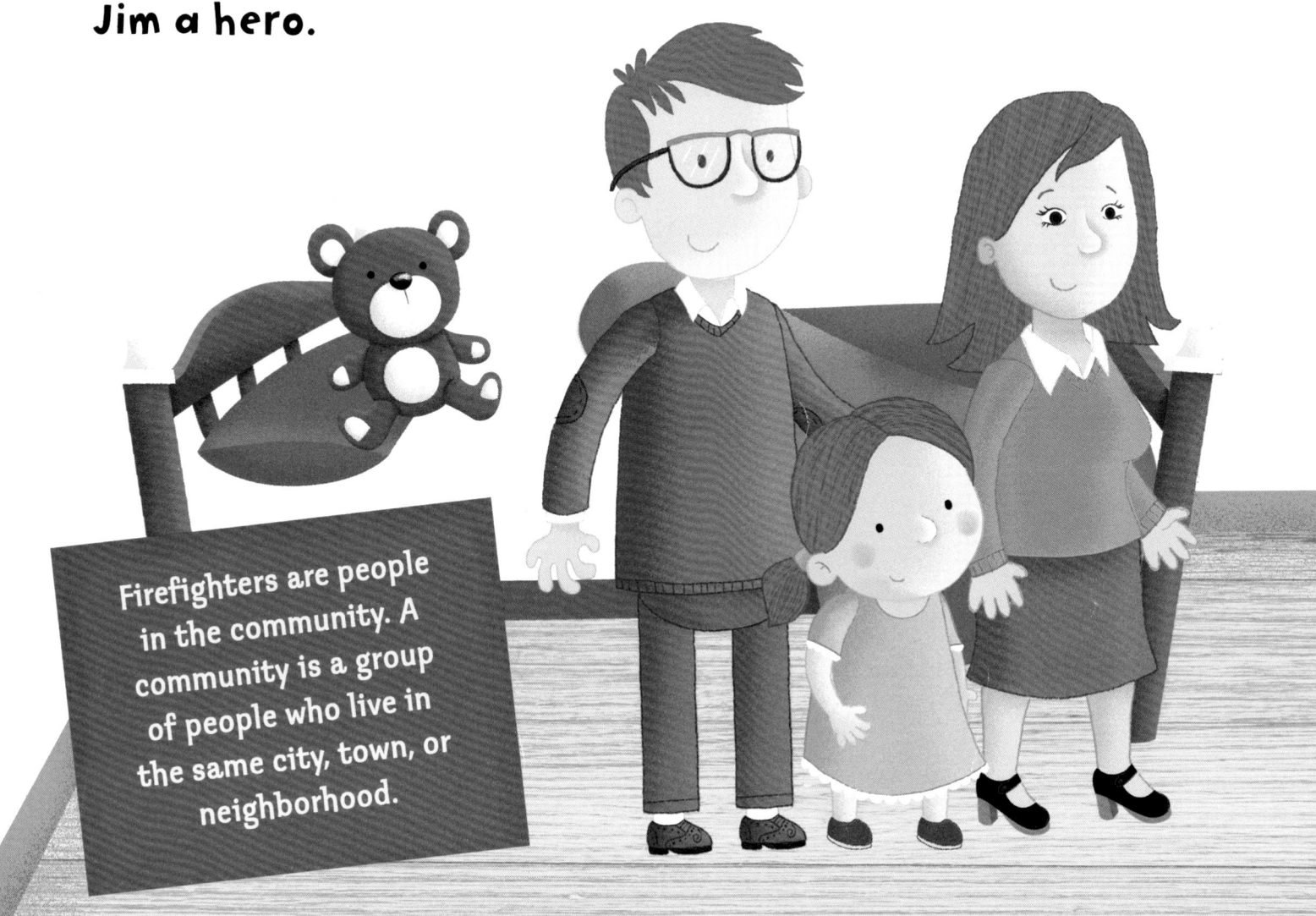

Firefighters are people in the community. A community is a group of people who live in the same city, town, or neighborhood.

Last week, Jim visited Gavin's home. He helped Gavin's family make a **fire escape plan.** The plan shows them how to escape if their home is ever on fire.

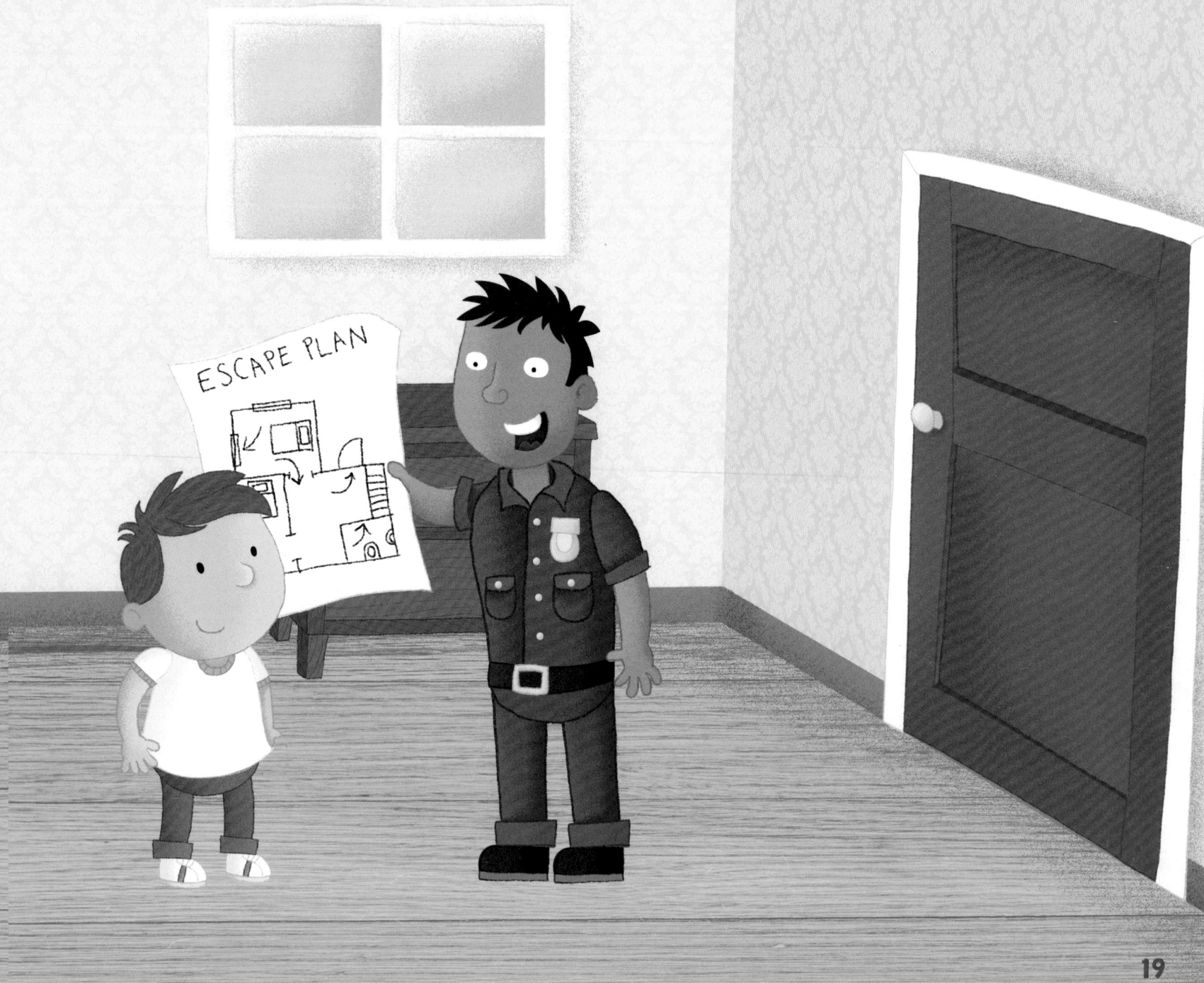

FIRE
SAFETY
WEEK

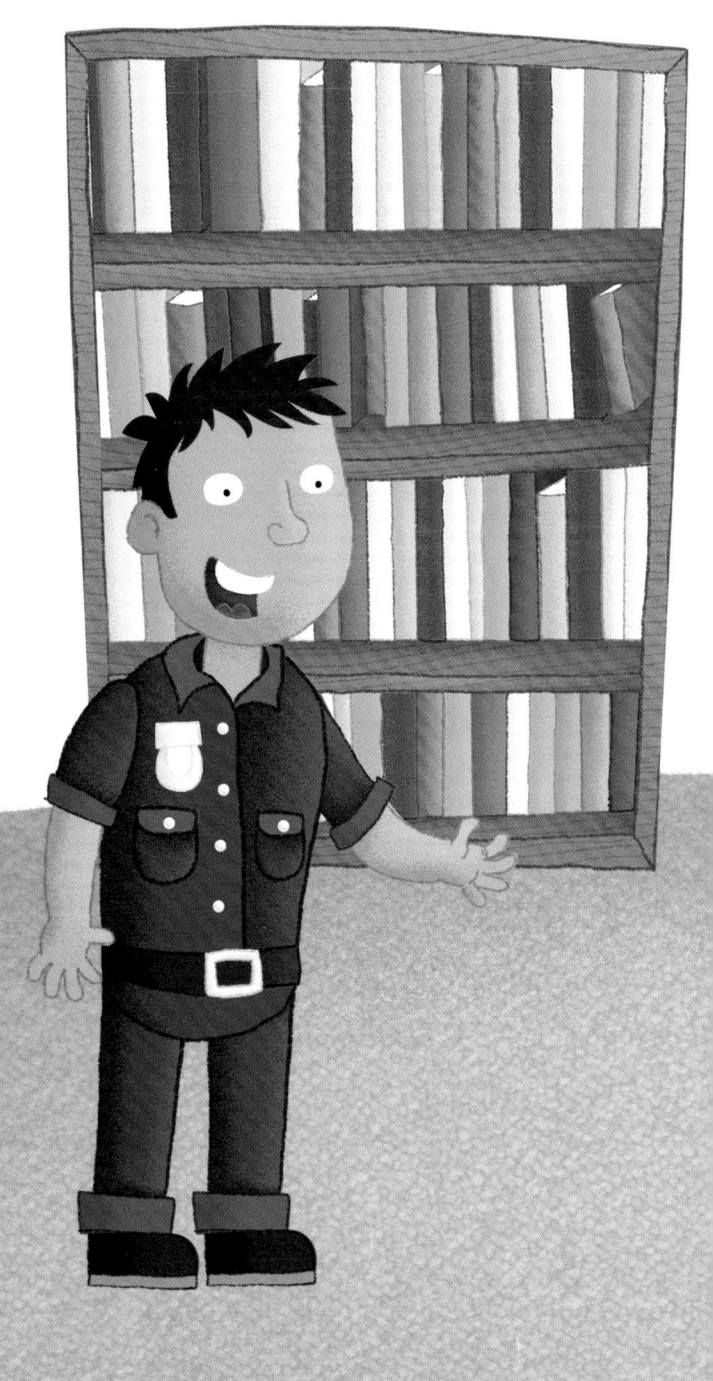

Firefighter Jim also visits schools. He came to our school during **Fire Safety Week.**

We practiced ways to escape a fire. And we learned how to prevent one.

Firefighter Jim gives us a hand with fire safety. So we give our safety helper a hand too!

Make a Fire Escape Plan

Firefighter Jim says a fire spreads fast. So firefighters plan their escape before they enter a burning building. Since a fire can happen at home, you should plan an escape too. Sit with your family and make a fire escape plan.

What you need:
one or more pieces of paper
a pencil

What to do:

1) On the paper, draw a map of the inside of your home. If your home has more than one floor, map out the other floors on separate sheets of paper. Label all rooms and show doors and windows. Mark the exits in each room with arrows. (If an exit is a window, keep a safety ladder in the room.) Next, pick a safe place outside where your family will meet. Choose a place in the front of your home but not too close to the house. It could be a mailbox, a light pole, or even a neighbor's porch. Draw an *X* on the paper to mark your safe meeting place.

2) Read the fire escape plan together. Practice using the plan during the day and at night. Have your own fire drill. Ask a grown-up to set off a smoke alarm. Leave the house through an exit. Meet at your safe meeting place. In a real fire, that's where you should call 9-1-1.

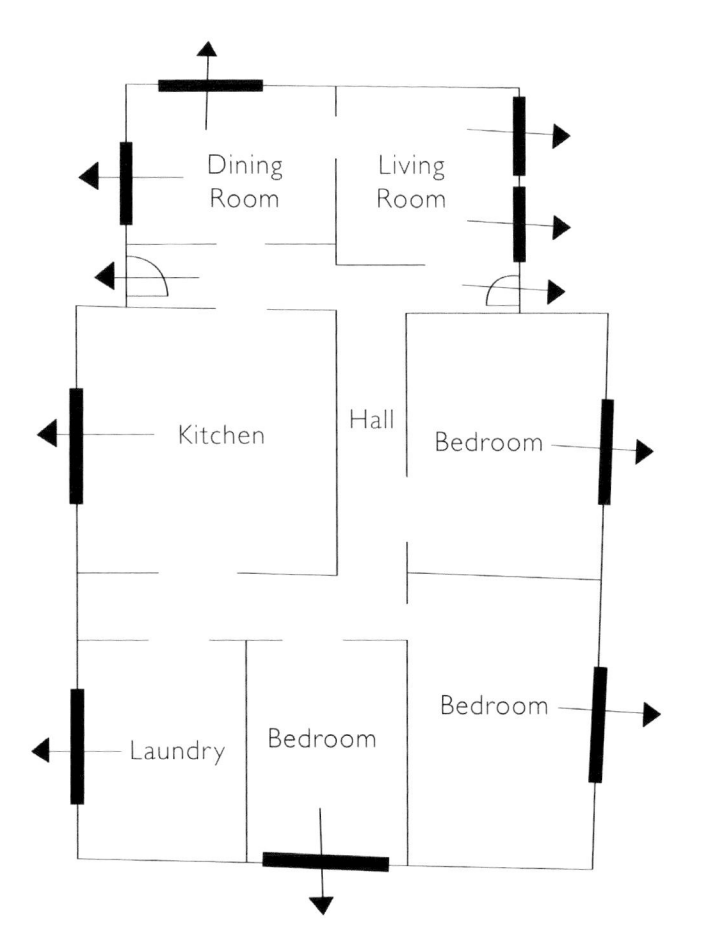

GLOSSARY

ambulance: an emergency vehicle that rushes sick or hurt people to the hospital

bunker gear: the safety clothes a firefighter wears in a fire

community: a group of people who live in the same area

emergencies: problems that need attention fast

exits: ways out of a home or building, such as doors and windows

fire escape plan: directions for how to escape a building that's on fire

fire hydrants: outdoor pipes that hold water for firefighters to use during a fire

first responders: rescue workers who are the first to arrive at an emergency

floods: high water on land that doesn't usually have water. Heavy rains can cause floods.

hook and ladder truck: another name for a fire truck

medical emergencies: health problems that need attention fast

oxygen: a substance in the air that people need to breathe

rescues: saves someone or something

smoke alarm: a small tool that makes a loud sound when smoke is near

traffic accidents: accidents that involve cars or other vehicles on the road

wounded: hurt

BOOKS

Gregory, Josh. *What Does it Do? Fire Truck.* Ann Arbor, MI: Cherry Lake Publishing, 2011.
Learn why a fire truck is an important firefighting tool.

Rau, Dana Meachen. *Firefighter.* New York: Marshall Cavendish, 2008.
Photos in this book show real firefighters putting on their gear and fighting fires.

Whiting, Sue. *The Firefighters.* Somerville, MA: Candlewick Press, 2010.
In this lively picture book, Mrs. Iverson's class gets a surprise visit from the local fire department.

WEBSITES

FireFacts
http://www.firefacts.org/
Meet firefighters Bill, Ashleigh, and Kevin, and learn about fire safety. You can also make a fire escape plan and play firefighting games.

Smokey Kids
http://www.smokeybear.com/kids/?js=1
Smokey the Bear from the U.S. Forest Service teaches you how to stop wildfires. Read campfire tips and make a story too.

Sparky
http://sparky.org/#/Sparky
This website is from the National Fire Prevention Association. It has lots of fun activities, cartoons, and a book about Sparky the Fire Dog.

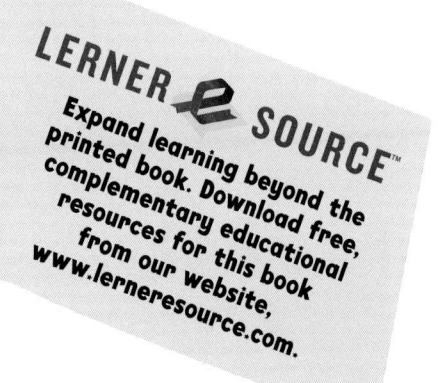

LERNER *e* SOURCE™
Expand learning beyond the printed book. Download free, complementary educational resources for this book from our website, www.lerneresource.com.